For Leah, Sally and
the whole Floris family.
Many thanks for all
your help and support – K.M.

This book belongs to

_____

Hello Scottish Animals!

Kate McLelland

K Picture Kelpies

Look at the Highland cows
munch, munch, munching.
Munching in the mountains.

Say hello to the cows!

Look at the red squirrels
leap, leap, leaping.
Leaping in the trees.

Say hello to the squirrels!

Look at the seals
swim, swim, swimming.
Swimming in the sea.

Say hello to the seals!

Look at the deer
run, run, running.
Running in the hills.

Say hello to the deer!

Look at the puffins
fish, fish, fishing.
Fishing by the cliffs.

Say hello to the puffins!

Look at the wildcats
climb, climb, climbing.
Climbing in the forest.

Say hello to the wildcats!

Look at the otters
play, play, playing.
Playing in the river.

Say hello to the otters!

Look at the dolphins
jump, jump, jumping.
Jumping in the waves.

Say hello to the dolphins!

Look at the Shetland ponies
trot, trot, trotting.
Trotting on the beach.

Say hello to the ponies!

Who can you spot
splash, splash, splashing?
Splashing in the loch.

Say hello to Nessie!